The Tiara Club

at Ruby Mansions

For the real Princess Chloe, and her lovely
mum, Queen Moira
VF

www.tiaraclub.co.uk

ORCHARD BOOKS
338 Euston Road, London NW1 3BH
Orchard Books Australia
Level 17/207 Kent St, Sydney NSW 2000

A Paperback Original
First published in Great Britain in 2007
Text © Vivian French 2007
Cover illustration © Sarah Gibb 2007
Inside illustrations © Orchard Books 2007

A CIP catalogue record for this book is available
from the British Library.

ISBN 978 1 84616 290 9

1 3 5 7 9 10 8 6 4 2

The paper and board used in this paperback are natural
recyclable products made from wood grown in sustainable
forests. The manufacturing processes conform to the
environmental regulations of the country of origin.

Orchard Books is a division of Hachette Children's Books

www.orchardbooks.co.uk

The Tiara Club

at Ruby Mansions

Princess Chloe

and the Primrose Petticoats

By Vivian French

ORCHARD BOOKS

The Royal Palace Academy
for the Preparation of Perfect Princesses

(Known to our students as "*The Princess Academy*")

OUR SCHOOL MOTTO:
*A Perfect Princess always thinks of others
before herself, and is kind, caring and truthful.*

**Ruby Mansions offers a complete education for
Tiara Club princesses with emphasis on the
creative arts. The curriculum includes:**

*Innovative Ideas for our
Friendship Festival*

*Ballet for Grace
and Poise*

*Designing Floral
Bouquets
(all thorns will be
removed)*

*A visit to the Diamond
Exhibition
(on the joyous occasion of
Queen Fabiola's birthday)*

**Our headteacher, Queen Fabiola, is present at all times,
and students are well looked after by the head fairy
godmother, Fairy G, and her assistant, Fairy Angora.**

Our resident staff and visiting experts include:

*KING BERNARDO IV
(Ruby Mansions Governor)*

*LADY HARRIS
(Secretary to Queen Fabiola)*

*LADY ARAMINTA
(Princess Academy Matron)*

*QUEEN MOTHER MATILDA
(Etiquette, Posture and
Flower Arranging)*

We award tiara points to encourage our Tiara Club princesses towards the next level. All princesses who win enough points at Ruby Mansions will attend a celebration ball, where they will be presented with their Ruby Sashes.

Ruby Sash Tiara Club princesses are invited to go on to Pearl Palace, our very special residence for Perfect Princesses, where they may continue their education at a higher level.

PLEASE NOTE:
Princesses are expected to arrive at
the Academy with a *minimum* of:

TWENTY BALLGOWNS
(with all necessary hoops,
petticoats, etc)

TWELVE DAY DRESSES

SEVEN GOWNS
suitable for garden parties,
and other special
day occasions

TWELVE TIARAS

DANCING SHOES
five pairs

VELVET SLIPPERS
three pairs

RIDING BOOTS
two pairs

Cloaks, muffs, stoles, gloves
and other essential
accessories as required

Oh, I'm SO excited!
I mean, here we are at Ruby Mansions,
learning to be Perfect Princesses –
isn't that just so AMAZING? And
you're here too – hurrah! I'm so
glad you can keep us company.
I'm Princess Chloe – have I told
you that? You might have met
the Rose Room Princesses
already – Charlotte, Katie,
Daisy, Alice, Sophia and Emily.
I'm in Poppy Room, and so are
Jessica, Georgia, Olivia, Lauren
and Amy – and we're ALL special
friends...and we're going to
have SUCH fun!

Chapter One

"What? What's that you say, child?" My new headteacher had her ear trumpet an inch from my nose. "Date, you say? What date? It's Monday today. First day of term!"

I took a deep breath and spoke as clearly as I could. "Please, Your Majesty, I'm sorry I'm LATE!"

Queen Fabiola jumped. "My dear!" she said. "There's no need to shout. A Perfect Princess NEVER raises her voice. And why are you late?"

I hung my head. I absolutely couldn't tell her the real reason. "I don't know," I mumbled.

"Slow? Your horses were too slow?" Queen Fabiola gave a sort of bark. I think she was laughing. "Dear me. If I've heard that excuse once, I've heard it a thousand times. Well, you're here now, so you'd better run along and find your friends. What did you say your name was?"

"Princess Chloe," I said, as loudly as I dared.

"Princess Zoe?" My headmistress looked puzzled. "I'm sure Princess Zoe arrived earlier. I didn't realise there were two of you. Never mind. I'll ask Lady Harris to check the lists later.

Do you know which dormitory you're in?"

I nodded. It seemed safer than trying to speak.

"Good, good. Run along, then." And Queen Fabiola waved me away with her ear trumpet.

I didn't mean to be late arriving at Ruby Mansions.

My mother's always busy doing queenly things, so my great-aunt looks after me – and she's very strict. She thinks I should wear plain satin gowns to make me look taller (I'm quite small for my age), but I just LOVE flowers and beads and embroidery, and loads and loads of fluffy net petticoats. I'm very lucky, because I have lots of girl cousins just a little bit older than me. They pass on their dresses when they grow out of them, and they're GORGEOUS!

My most favourite dress ever is a fabulous pale forget-me-not blue, with gathered skirts so you can see the petticoats underneath – and would you believe it? The petticoats are sewn all over with tiny yellow primroses. Honestly, when I first saw it I thought I would die of excitement! But do you know what my great-aunt said? She said it was too flowery, and I wasn't to wear it. But I just knew it would be absolutely perfect for the Ruby Mansions beginning-of-term ball.

And that was why I was late. I had to wait until my

great-aunt had gone downstairs to talk to the coachman. As soon as she'd gone, I threw open my trunk and squeezed in my primrose petticoat dress, and all the other pretty ones as well.

It was a TERRIBLE squash (I am SO not good at packing!), and there were some papers and cards that got in the way, so I shoved them under my bed. My great-aunt kept calling me to hurry up and come downstairs, but she never guessed what I was doing.

Chapter Two

It took me a while to find my way to the dormitories. I wandered round the corridors a bit, and then I met Fairy G. She was puffing along with a pile of notebooks, but she stopped when she saw me.

"Aha! Princess Chloe!" she said. "Welcome to Ruby Mansions!"

"Please Fairy G," I asked, "can you tell me where Poppy Room is?"

"Through the glass doors, across the ballroom, and up the stairs at the end." Fairy G told me. "Rose Room is on the right, and Poppy Room is on the left."

And she beamed, and puffed away, dropping things as she went. Fairy G's the most important fairy godmother in the Princess Academy. Sometimes we see her, and sometimes we see her deputy, Fairy Angora, but they both look after us. Fairy G's good fun. I think she's my favourite teacher.

The stairs wound round and round, but at last I couldn't go any further. In front of me were two doors. I peeped cautiously inside the first one – and I STARED. It was so pretty. Roses cascaded over the wallpaper, and there were roses embroidered on the bedspreads. Charlotte, Katie, Daisy, Alice, Sophia and Emily were busy unpacking their boxes and trunks, and when they saw me they waved cheerfully.

"Isn't this the most HEAVENLY Rose Room?" Alice said. "Go and see Poppy Room! You'll LOVE it!"

I hurried next door – it was GORGEOUS. Pink, red and white poppies were scattered

everywhere – even the carpet had a poppy design. And then I saw my friends piled on a couple of beds at the far end, chattering and laughing.

"Hi! I called. "I'm here!"

Have you ever been hugged by five friends at once? It was lovely!

"We were wondering when you'd arrive," Georgia said. "We were beginning to get worried!" And she gave me a little extra hug.

"What do you think of our dormitory?" Olivia asked.

"It's WONDERFUL," I said. "It's not a bit like our room in Silver Towers."

Jessica grinned. "And our new headteacher isn't a bit like Queen Samantha Joy. Have you met her yet?"

"Yes," I said. "She's VERY deaf, isn't she? She thinks my name is Princess Zoe."

Lauren and Amy began to giggle. "She thought I was called Mamie, and Lauren was called Maureen!" Amy told me. "We had to show her our invitations before she got it right."

A cold feeling hit my stomach, as if I'd swallowed a lump of ice. "Invitations?" I said feebly.

Georgia jumped up and ran to

her bedside table. She came back waving a gold embossed card, with a huge crown on the top.

As Georgia read it out, the ice lump in my stomach grew bigger and bigger as I realised what I'd done. The invitation was in the middle of the papers I'd shoved under my bed!

His Most Royal Highness King Bernardo the Fourth, Governor of Ruby Mansions, wishes to invite Princess Georgia to a ball in his illustrious Gilded Ballroom in order to celebrate the beginning of a new term at Ruby Mansions

Please keep your invitation and present it on arrival in order to be admitted.

"Chloe! You've gone pale!" Olivia said. "Are you all right?"

"No," I said. "I haven't got my invitation!"

Chapter Three

My friends told me it wouldn't matter, but I knew it did. It was such a bad way to begin my very first day at Ruby Mansions.

"Go and see Fairy G," Lauren suggested.

I nodded. "I'll go now."

"I'll come with you," Jessica said, jumping up.

We were crossing the ballroom
when we saw Diamonde and
Gruella, the horrible twins,
coming towards us. Gruella looked
very upset – her eyes were red,
and she was blowing her nose.

Even though none of us Poppy Roomers like her very much we stopped to ask if she was all right.

"No, I'm not," she sniffed. "One of our trunks has gone missing, and it's got ALL my ballgowns in it!"

"That's TERRIBLE," I said. "I'm so sorry."

"Have you told Fairy G?" Jessica asked.

Diamonde tossed her head. "Of course she has. She's not stupid, like SOME people! Come on, Gruella!" And she stormed off, dragging Gruella behind her.

Jessica and I looked after them.

"Why does Diamonde always have to be so horrid?" I asked.

Jessica shrugged. "Who knows? Let's find Fairy G!"

We went through the ballroom, and into the corridor. There were loads of doors, but none of them had any names on them.

"Maybe we should just knock on one," Jessica suggested. "Go on, Chloe – choose a door!"

I looked round. "That one!" I said, and we marched towards it.

Jessica knocked, and a voice called, "Come in!"

My heart sank. It was Queen Fabiola – our headmistress.

Of course we had to go in. Queen Fabiola was sitting behind a golden desk, and her assistant sat on a small chair beside her.

"Why, it's Princess Jessica and the second Princess Zoe!" Queen Fabiola looked at me over the top of her glasses. "Lady Harris, I don't think you've met this Princess Zoe."

I began to curtsey to Lady Harris, but I caught my foot, and fell over.

I felt SO silly as I got to my feet, and Queen Fabiola frowned.

"Really, Princess Zoe! You MUST learn to behave a little more like a Perfect Princess!" She pointed her ear trumpet at Jessica and me. "Well? What was it you wanted?"

I didn't know whether to ask where Fairy G was, or to tell her about my invitation, so I said nothing.

"Come along, child – come along!" Queen Fabiola began to tap on her desk.

I gulped. "I'm very sorry, Your Majesty," I said, "but I've lost my invitation to the Ruby Mansions beginning-of-term ball."

This time Queen Fabiola looked stern. VERY stern.

"I can forgive one mistake, Princess Zoe," she said. "I can even forgive two. But you seem determined to get yourself into trouble. I will consider the matter of your missing invitation. Please come back tomorrow morning!"

Chapter Four

I felt TERRIBLE! And as Jessica and I walked out, Diamonde and Gruella were waiting outside. Diamonde gave us a superior look.

"In trouble already?" she asked. "Fancy that!"

"So why are YOU here?" Jessica asked.

Gruella made a face. "Fairy G told me to come and tell Queen Fabiola about my trunk."

"Oh dear!" I couldn't help feeling sorry for her, even if she wasn't very nice.

"I do hope it comes in time for the ball," she said, and she sounded really anxious. "Diamonde's got a GORGEOUS dress to wear, but I haven't got anything!"

"Couldn't Diamonde lend you one of her other dresses?" Jessica suggested.

Diamonde gave Jessica SUCH a despising stare. "ALL my other dresses are packed with Gruella's!"

"Diamonde made SUCH a fuss about her best dress being squashed," Gruella said. "She moaned and MOANED until Mummy packed it in a special box for her."

Diamonde smiled a horribly self-satisfied smile. "You see?" she said. "I was right!"

"But I didn't know our trunk was going to get lost!" Gruella wailed.

"POOR you." I tried to think of a way to make her feel better. "You can have one of my dresses, if you like. I've got heaps and heaps!"

I knew I'd made a mistake as soon as I'd finished speaking. I could see from the twins' faces they thought I was being a horrible show-off.

"Thank you, gracious princess," Diamonde said, and she sounded SO sarcastic.

Gruella sneered. "Who's a lucky little princess, then?"

"I didn't mean it to sound like that," I began, but it was too late.

Diamonde opened Queen Fabiola's door, and she and Gruella flounced through.

Jessica squeezed my arm. "Just ignore them."

But I couldn't. A little bit of me really did feel sorry for Gruella. I kept remembering how sad she'd looked in the ballroom, and I did SO know how she must be feeling about the ball. I'd been miserable when I thought I'd have to wear one of my satin dresses. It would be TERRIBLE to have no dress at all!

When Jessica and I got back to Poppy Room we found Lauren waiting for us.

"Hi!" she said cheerfully. "Everyone else has gone down to tea. Have you sorted out your invitation?"

I shook my head. "I've got to see Queen Fabiola tomorrow morning."

"I'm sure it'll be all right." Lauren patted my arm. "Oh – have you heard? The twins have lost their luggage!"

"We met them downstairs," Jessica said. "They're just as ghastly as ever."

"Gruella might have been grumpy because she hasn't got any ballgowns," I suggested.

"*A Perfect Princess always thinks the best of others,*" Jessica quoted. "You're a perfect princess, Chloe. Come on. We'd better not be late for tea."

*

After tea was over, we were sent back to our rooms to unpack our trunks. I felt SO much better when I pulled out my dress with the primrose petticoats, and the whole of Poppy Room *ooohed* and *aaaahed* in amazement.

"You'll be the belle of the ball!" Olivia told me as I hung it on the front of my wardrobe.

"If I'm allowed to go," I said.

"Of course you will be," Georgia said firmly.

There was a knock on the door, and Gruella waltzed in, with Diamonde close behind her. Gruella didn't look upset any more. She looked as if she was on top of the world.

"I've come to choose my dress," she announced. "The carrier took my trunk away by mistake, and it won't be back until next week."

As my friends stared in astonishment, Diamonde gave us a sneery smile. "Aren't we SO lucky that Chloe has HEAPS of dresses, and can spare one for poor little Gruella?"

And then Gruella saw my dress with the primrose petticoats

hanging on the wardrobe. She gave a little gasp, and my stomach lurched.

I just KNEW what she was going to say...and she said it.

"I'll have THAT dress." And she marched towards it.

I couldn't move.

"But that's Chloe's special dress for King Bernardo's ball," Amy protested.

Gruella swung round, her eyebrows raised.

"What do you say, Chloe? Can I have this one? After all, you do have HEAPS of them…"

"That's right," Diamonde agreed. "Heaps and HEAPS! And you did say Gruella could have one!"

Chapter Five

What could I say? I HAD offered Gruella a dress. And it would sound SO horrible to say she couldn't have that one after I'd sounded so boastful. I swallowed hard.

"That's fine," I said. "I...I really hope you enjoy wearing it."

"Oh, I WILL," Gruella said, and

just for a second she looked really happy. And then she, Diamonde and the dress were gone.

"WOW!" Lauren said loudly. "You're an ANGEL, Chloe. I'd never have let her walk off with my very best dress like that!"

"What are you going to wear now?" Georgia asked.

I sat down on my bed. I felt a bit sick. "I'm not sure," I said. "I'll decide tomorrow. When I know I'm actually going to go to the ball."

I didn't sleep very well that night. I kept counting all the things that had gone wrong. I'd been late arriving, the headmistress didn't like me, I was too scared to tell her my real name, I might not be allowed to go to King Bernardo's ball...and Gruella had my beautiful BEAUTIFUL primrose petticoat dress.

I told myself a Perfect Princess should be glad she'd done such a Good Deed, but it didn't make me feel any better. Not one bit. By the time the alarm bell rang, I was worn out. I crept out of bed, and although Georgia and Jessica tried their best to cheer me up, I couldn't eat any breakfast.

We were about to clear our plates when Fairy G came sailing into the dining hall.

"Good morning, everybody!" she boomed. "Now, I have to tell you of a change in arrangements.

Queen Fabiola feels that one or two of you have forgotten how to curtsey, and to behave as Perfect Princesses should. She is concerned that you will not appear at your best at King Bernardo's ball."

Fairy G didn't look at me, but I could feel my face burning.

"So this morning," Fairy G went on, "we're to have a dress rehearsal. Run upstairs and put on your ballgowns, and hurry to the ballroom. Queen Fabiola and I will meet you there."

Everyone was thrilled – except me. They flew up to the

dormitories, and by the time I walked slowly into Poppy Room it was a froth of skirts and petticoats.

"What are you going to wear, Chloe?" Jessica was struggling with

her sash, and Lauren was helping her. They both looked FABULOUS. Jessica had the loveliest dress covered in sparkly silver stars, and Lauren was wearing the most luscious pink velvet.

I went to my wardrobe. I'd packed my pretty dresses so badly they were all creased, and looked horrid. I pulled out one of the satin ones instead.

When I'd put it on I looked in the mirror, and I nearly cried. Everyone else had stars or sparkles or lace, and my dress was SO plain. It was too big, as well – my great-aunt thought it would last longer that way.

"You look very pretty," Georgia said, but I knew she was just being kind.

Chapter Six

The ballroom was already full of princesses when we arrived, and I felt worse and worse. Queen Fabiola was standing on a platform at one end, and Fairy G boomed at us to hurry up. I tried to sneak into the back row, but Queen Fabiola beckoned to me.

"Ah! Princess Zoe! Come to the front. I'm particularly anxious about you. I want to see if it's possible for you to curtsey without falling over."

Of course that made me even more nervous. Fairy G gave me an encouraging wink, but I couldn't smile back.

"Let us begin!" Queen Fabiola ordered. "Step right, left foot behind, head up, and CURTSEY! Oh – EXCELLENT, Princess Olivia! ENCHANTING, Princess Gruella!" She paused, and I thought she was going to tell me off again, but she was looking past me. "Come here, Gruella my dear. Perhaps you and Olivia could demonstrate how a curtsey SHOULD be performed!"

And there was Gruella, in my dress with the primrose petticoats, pushing her way to the front. She and Olivia turned to face us, and as they turned their backs on

Fairy G and Queen Fabiola I saw
Fairy G's eyes open wide. Queen
Fabiola began to speak – then
stopped, and stared.

"Gruella, my DEAREST child!
Your dress! It's truly lovely – but it
isn't done up!" She peered more
closely at it. "Didn't you tell me
your ballgowns had gone astray?
Where has this dress come from?
It does seem a little too small
for you..."

Before Gruella could say
anything, Olivia dropped yet
another of her brilliant curtsies.
"Please, Your Majesty," she said,
and her voice was very clear.

"Princess Chloe lent it to her. It's Chloe's very best dress, but she felt so sorry for Princess Gruella she said she could wear it."

Queen Fabiola looked pleased, but confused. "How kind of Princess Chloe," she said. "That is a truly generous gesture." She gazed over my head at the princesses behind me. "Will Princess Chloe please step forward?"

I took a deep breath, stepped forward, and sank into my very best curtsey ever.

"What's this? What? WHAT?" Our headmistress looked SO muddled that Fairy G took pity on her.

"I think," she boomed, "there has been some confusion. This is Princess Chloe, Your Majesty, and she is, as I know well, the kindest of princesses. I would also suggest there has been some confusion about the dresses..."

And Fairy G winked at me, and waved her wand.

The air was so filled with sparkly fairy dust we all began to sneeze...and when we'd stopped sneezing, there I was in my GORGEOUS dress with the primrose petticoats, and Gruella

was wearing my satin dress! And do you know what? She looked absolutely beautiful! Every princess in the ballroom began to clap, and Queen Fabiola waved her ear trumpet at me.

"Well done, Princess Chloe! And I do apologise for calling you by the wrong name, my dear. Lady Harris, could we find Princess Chloe an invitation to King Bernardo's ball?"

Lady Harris smiled at me. "Of course," she said.

Chapter Seven

King Bernardo's beginning of term ball was SO fabulous! We were taken there in the Ruby Mansions coaches, which are gold, with the most luxurious ruby-red velvet cushions. King Bernardo took our invitations, and then kissed our hands – and he told me I looked beautiful! I blushed BRIGHT red, but I didn't care. I was wearing my dress with the primrose petticoats, and I was with my lovely friends.

We danced and DANCED!

When the coaches came to take us home, Diamonde and Gruella were in our coach, and Gruella actually smiled at me.

"Thank you for the dress," she said.

"You look wonderful in it,"

I said, and I meant every word. "PLEASE keep it."

"OK," Gruella said, and she gave me a funny little sideways look. "I'll say yes, because I know you've got loads and LOADS of other dresses."

And I still don't know if she was being sly or not. But I don't mind, because Ruby Mansions is SO fantastic...

and I'm SO happy here...

and I'll see you SOON!

What happens next?
Find out in

Princess Jessica
and the **Best-Friend Bracelet**

Hi! It's me! Princess Jessica!
And it's lovely to meet you, and to
know you're here at Ruby Mansions with
me and my friends from Poppy Room.
Have you met us all? As well as me
there's Chloe, Olivia, Lauren,
Georgia and Amy. And Charlotte,
Katie, Daisy, Alice, Sophia and
Emily are in Rose Room right next
door to us. Things would be just about
perfect if only those horrible twins,
Diamonde and Gruella weren't
here - they get worse and worse,
especially Diamonde!

The Tiara Club

Have you met the Rose Room princesses?

PRINCESS CHARLOTTE
AND THE **BIRTHDAY BALL**
ISBN 978 1 84362 863 7

PRINCESS KATIE
AND THE **SILVER PONY**
ISBN 978 1 84362 860 6

PRINCESS DAISY
AND THE **DAZZLING DRAGON**
ISBN 978 1 84362 864 4

PRINCESS ALICE
AND THE **MAGICAL MIRROR**
ISBN 978 1 84362 861 3

PRINCESS SOPHIA
AND THE **SPARKLING SURPRISE**
ISBN 978 1 84362 862 0

PRINCESS EMILY
AND THE **BEAUTIFUL FAIRY**
ISBN 978 1 84362 859 0

And been with them at Silver Towers?

PRINCESS CHARLOTTE
AND THE **ENCHANTED ROSE**
ISBN 978 1 84616 195 7

PRINCESS KATIE
AND THE **DANCING BROOM**
ISBN 978 1 84616 196 4

PRINCESS DAISY
AND THE MAGICAL MERRY-GO-ROUND
ISBN 978 1 84616 197 1

PRINCESS ALICE
AND THE **CRYSTAL SLIPPER**
ISBN 978 1 84616 198 8

PRINCESS SOPHIA
AND THE **PRINCE'S PARTY**
ISBN 978 1 84616 199 5

PRINCESS EMILY
AND THE **WISHING STAR**
ISBN 978 1 84616 200 8

Win a Tiara Club Perfect Princess Prize!

Look for the secret word in mirror writing that is hidden in a tiara in each of the Tiara Club books. Each book has one word. Put together the six words from books **13** to **18** to make a special Perfect Princess sentence, then send it to us together with 20 words or more on why you like the Tiara Club books. Each month, we will put the correct entries in a draw and one lucky reader will receive a magical Perfect Princess prize!

Send your Perfect Princess sentence, at least 20 words on why you like the Tiara Club, your name and your address on a postcard to:
THE TIARA CLUB COMPETITION,
Orchard Books, 338 Euston Road,
London, NW1 3BH

Australian readers should write to:
Hachette Children's Books,
Level 17/207 Kent Street, Sydney, NSW 2000.

Only one entry per child.
Final draw: 31 May 2008

Look out for

Butterfly Ball

with Princess Amy and Princess Olivia!
ISBN 978 1 84616 470 5

And look out for the Lily Room princesses in
the Tiara Club at Pearl Palace:

Princess Hannah and the Little Black Kitten
Princess Isabella and the Snow-White Swan
Princess Lucy and the Precious Puppy
Princess Grace and the Golden Nightingale
Princess Ellie and the Enchanted Fawn
Princess Sarah and the Silver Swan

By Vivian French
Illustrated by Sarah Gibb
The Tiara Club

The Tiara Club at Silver Towers

The Tiara Club at Ruby Mansions

All priced at £3.99.
Christmas Wonderland and *Butterfly Ball* are priced at £5.99.
The Tiara Club books are available from all good bookshops, or can be ordered direct
from the publisher: Orchard Books, PO BOX 29, Douglas IM99 IBQ.
Credit card orders please telephone 01624 836000 or fax 01624 837033 or visit our
website: www.wattspub.co.uk or e-mail: bookshop@enterprise.net for details.

To order please quote title, author, ISBN and your full name and address.
Cheques and postal orders should be made payable to 'Bookpost plc.'
Postage and packing is FREE within the UK
(overseas customers should add £2.00 per book).

Prices and availability are subject to change.

Check out

The Tiara Club

website at:

www.tiaraclub.co.uk

You'll find Perfect Princess games and fun things to do, as well as news on the Tiara Club and all your favourite princesses!